Let's Play Tag!

 Read the Page

Read the Story

Repeat

Stop

Game

Level 1 Level 2 Level 3

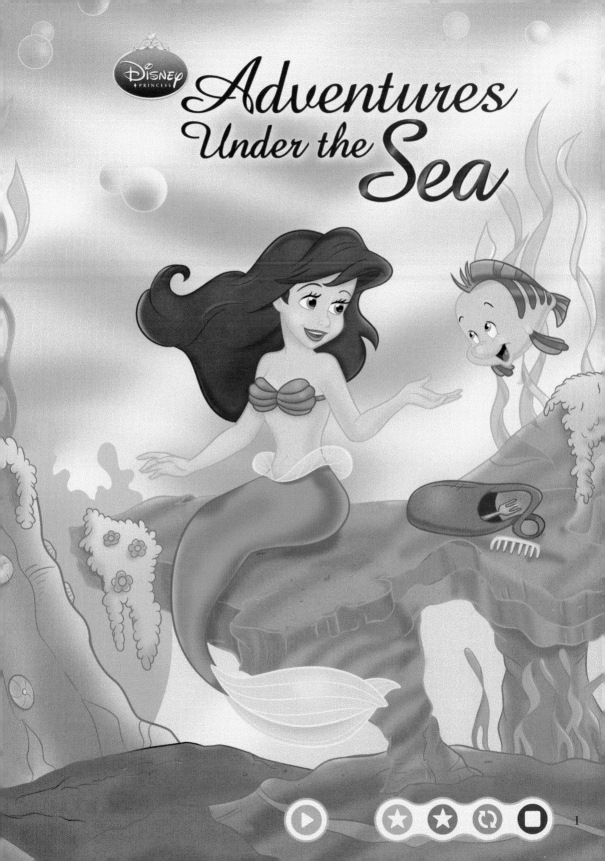

Adventures
Under the
Sea

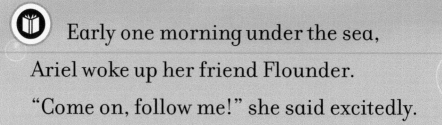 Early one morning under the sea,
Ariel woke up her friend Flounder.
"Come on, follow me!" she said excitedly.

Flounder yawned. "Sure, but where are we going Ariel?"

Ariel smiled. "It's a surprise!"

 "Flounder, hurry up!" Ariel called.

"You know I can't swim that fast," Flounder panted.

Ariel led Flounder to a big, sunken boat. "Isn't it fantastic?"

Flounder was not sure. The boat looked dark inside. "Let's get out of here!" he said nervously.

"You're not getting cold fins now, are you?" asked Ariel.

"Who me?" Flounder stuttered. "No way!"

The boat was full of human treasures! Something shiny caught Ariel's eye.

"Oh my gosh!" Ariel gasped.
"Have you ever seen anything so
wonderful in your entire life?!"

"Wow! Cool!" Flounder exclaimed.
"But uh, what is it?"

Ariel shrugged, "I don't know."

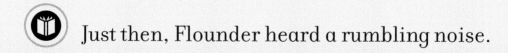 Just then, Flounder heard a rumbling noise.

"Did you hear something?" he whispered.

But Ariel didn't hear him. She was busy
collecting treasures.

"I wonder what this is?"

Suddenly, a big shark burst through the boat! "Shark! Shark!" Flounder shouted. "Swim! A shark!"

Ariel and Flounder swam

for their lives.

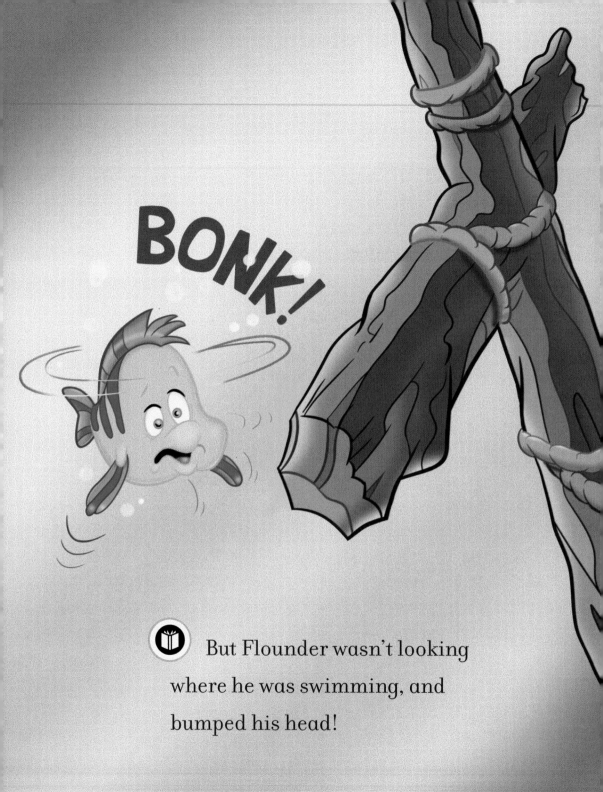

But Flounder wasn't looking
where he was swimming, and
bumped his head!

He suddenly felt very dizzy.
Instead of swimming, he
was sinking!

Ariel looked back and saw
her friend falling.
"Flounder!" she called.

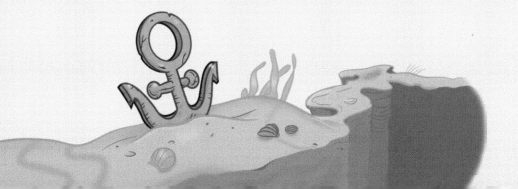

Ariel swam as fast as she could and caught Flounder.

Then, just when the shark was about to catch them both, he got caught instead!

Flounder stuck his tongue out at the shark.

"You big bully!"

As they swam away, Flounder asked,
"That was really scary—right Ariel?"

"Oh Flounder, don't be such a guppy,"
Ariel joked.

"I am not a guppy!" Flounder answered.
"But could your next surprise, maybe, not
include sharks?"

Ariel and Flounder laughed as they raced
all the way back home.

cup

box

rip

u

pin

nut

bug

wig

dog

lid

tub

mop

pot

o

i

frame

trumpet

prince

drum

princess

dr
br
tr
fr
pr

tree

fruit

tray

drink

braid

dress

bracelet

pomegranate

lemon

peanut

apple

banana

melon

orange

pear

S

pomegranates

lemons

peanuts

apples

bananas

melons

oranges

pears

Jasmine Discovers the World

palace

Sphinx

Arabian horses

caravan

oasis

Cupid

temple

fountain

grove

pyramids